Dead Starships

poems

by

Wendy Rathbone

Dear Starships
Poems by Wendy Rathbone
Copyright © 2016 by Wendy Rathbone
Published by Eye Scry Publications
www.eyescrypublications.com
All Rights Reserved

ISBN: 978-1-942415-12-1
Eye Scry Publications

Many other Eye Scry Publications are available at a substantial volume discount to bookstores, libraries, etc. Please visit our website at www.eyescrypublications.com

Piracy ruins lives!

"And thought also of the drowned star city, of the dead starships."

--S.P. Somtow, "I Wake from a Dream of a Drowned Star City."

Part One

Starshiptopia

*I watch the red lights of
dead starships
gather among the old stars*

Distances

a ship full of stars
a winter galaxy of snow
moving upon the blackwing dark
onyx cold
deeplight years of solitude
the blue stone memory of Earth
the green glaze of dawn
the black umbrella of night
bracken rivers, rain, silver seas
windows candled orange
poem-leaf windblown upon the silk
horizon
a prehistoric moon quivers
in partitions of amber-thick shadows
melting against the glass panes
stark possessive love
bodiless, airless, lightless
in the starship of my rooms between stars
I can hear a simmering storm
ion fresh
so far away
from this dream of the distances I travel

The Future

auburn droids
serve
moon-tea
steam rising as far as
Swarovski stars

The Martian Doll

Sitting upon the red stone her hair of iridium and the berserker eyes of enlarged atoms lips of rose dust the high nose of a queen from a bluer century about a billion turns ago what child thrilled to dress her in pink hologram robes and suits to match the alien skies her body of synthetic foam that never decays rendering her neither ragged nor limp an un-aged artifact of the dry sea bottom her memory still charged her smile all-knowing.

On the Mantle

a jar full of crystals labeled: *stars*

Kindling

Autumn is a town
  on its own star
fallen from
  the coldest
    constellation

Weird Stories I Should Write

Of variable pearls
and wolf journeys
Time-travelers listing consequences
Star-maids dying...

The lost boys are back
lifting a thousand veils
exposing dragons and
Babylonian knowledge

The spirit between
art and thrill
resides in midnight woods (or Mars)
Monarchs, flutes, harps,
black skies, final roses
a mixture of summer and bone...

Friends recommend starships
and dark equations
but I prefer love
and all its ghosts
even if its cold silver slipper
is a tight fit

The Sea

The tide is night
The sea swims with planets
And schools of moons
Finned rockets slide through the murk
Impossible void-maids
Comb their nebulae hair

Before My Father Vanished

in the Blacksun Nebulas
he gave me
a string of mooncrystals
in cool ambers
and the rogue purple-pinks
of
lost stars
I wore them to bed
and
in the shower
for twenty lunar years
and to work in the rocket yards
where they failed to warm
amid bittersmoke and cinder
even elements of the cold beyond

under the jet and glare and noise
one night they broke--
scattered light across
the gravel landing field
I found only a handful
ten unthawed cubes
ten unleashed winter suns
my father's stardust
remains

How To Mine Moonlight

set a thousand mirrors facing upward
hold aloft a basket made of satin and
straw
line all your trees with hooks
leave quartz crystals and amethyst
                in the garden
become a meteor treading the tides of
space

Build a Rocketship Contest: Alternative Class A Instructions and Suggestions

Section One

it shall please the wind
if you make your rockets
of silk and balsa
for this journey is not about
functionality
it is all emotion
how trembled sands
and vortex seas
make a language
in the shape of yearning
how the wings of your
star-boat flicker
to a thrill
more about the hunter
less about the hunt

Section Two

Past winners include rockets made of
magnetic poems
and Victorian lanterns
a candle in every porthole

your vessel may run on the fuel of wine
trailing fumes of oakmoss and patchouli
you will be rated on the colors of
its vapors
how well they curve and twine
in pink torrents or Mediterranean blue
and if the black fog of the thrusters
can be distilled to ink
for the old parchment logbooks
your captain will require

Section Three

your final judges—
all former starship commanders
who have suffered the inexorable
isolation of space

Crash Landed On

a planet called Lone
made of dogs barking in the distance
made of saffron wind

After the Star War

Starship junkyard. The ghosts there are
rusting. Their horror of orbital decay. The
freighter blew up.
We could see the fires back of Mars. The
blast-scarred starwarships. The once great
armada.

Relics float. Marooned. Picking up
classical music from subspace. So many
dead ships.
So many hearts of darkness.

During the war the timeslips leeched
all color. All but the blue novas of your
eyes. All censored but your gaze. And
war's collapsing madness.

It was ultra misery. Drugged
complacence.
Deliriums of hate. Hating the stars.
Yelling for change and heroes.
Learning why rebels shoot at suns.

You had that rakish look. Dreams
of survival. Then taking the lead. But
when the destruction began, and

moonfires caressed your hair, you went
running backward all changed of mind.

Well, this is the Black that Jack built. The
lonely everlasting suck. The tumble. The
tremble. The abyss and the scream.
Physicists, poets cannot tell the difference.

You watched the midlands for comets.
For agents of lightyear ruins. You
soon learned that garden-variety
astronauts despise vertigo. Disorder.
Absolute zero.

Only the prophet profits from war.
Lazerguns ™ at 80 mil.

What you faced? Quasars on the brink of
death.
Amorphous anti-heroes. Spacewrecks.
Floating empty void-fear.

Finally it was time to stop the fight. The
hate.
Learn to acclimate. Planet-lock.
Time to make a home.

You defected. Picked a world. Picked a
time.

Learned to love. My alien refugee.

World Of

world of enclosed bubble cities from a
science fiction book cover

world of orange vacuums behind dead
trees

world of cold giants with beards of frost

world of Alexanders conquering
themselves with the sun in their hair

world of time's incandescent windows
leading to portals of every possibility

world of rice and grain and warm peach
days in dreaming eyes

world of endless crossroads that make
everything plaid

world of October fusions harnessing the
energy of leaves

world of rails of light like never-ending
trains of tears

world of hidden faces sleeping in the
foliage

world of temperate hearts unmaking love

world of sugar cottages and bears who
are men

world of tentacles streaming into any
available orifice

world of open air and the angels who nest
there

world of gravity tender and ancient as the
dark

Homecoming

the rocket falling
all the years of stars collected in pearly
pools
rush by as the white egret turns
to watch
in this melted dawn
our swift return to Earth

homecoming means
new hugs new breath new minutes
to lie down in
the grass of rivers and antiquity

I missed the wind the most
green lightning fog and
billion year old salt and sea
I breathe
I breathe the deep dust
the fresh and the dead the moths the
beach
exhale hometown words: bougainvillea
San Diego, strawberry

sharing
French wine
the cologne of summer
the lacy languages of insects
in moon-lit rooms

the blue emerging shadows
come
imbibing and elongating the hours
to an infinite moment
of awakening
beyond
that frozen journey
the evening served on tables of clouds
over
elegant draperies of rain

I am home

galaxies at my windows
a warm gold bed
my favorite fevers wash over me
my sleep amid warm drops of light
turning in damp air
to see
autumn rockets
lining the dusk
red and humming
sweet acid burn
of
their spiral trails
I breathe the far-fire scent
and dream
star-boats festering above
a metal dawn

Hanging Out at the Space Docks

under the spaceport's verdant sky
all the golden ships line up
to land
but the big star-boats dock beyond
the thin exosphere
sometimes
I go up to the orbiting quays
to hear the gossip of pirates
and watch the winding blue sparks
of the warp trails
the spacers all have drugged eyes
and frosted hair
coming from the night
that eternally ingests them
coming out of the madness
the seven seas of stars

Space-Wine Tasting

this vintage was aged in space, she said

I taste a hint of leaf-time
a touch of blue-salt Earthiness
astral-flecked godliness
ripened on the vinegars of sour moons
and in the silt
the barest edge of ash
reminds me of the first seeder ships
that warped out and burned
from within
the flavor trembles
with their ancient breath

Layover

Mars is a plum in the sky
late summer
the scent of rockets burns in your hair
our time together is short
the air of alien worlds
carries through the open door
there is no space between us
only an entire void
when you leave again
remember to shut the window
the nights are getting colder
and the departing shuttles
keep me awake at night

A New Design

when they made the starships
look like swans
I realized
a poet had designed them
They took flight
over ponds of snowmoons
as meteors clung
to the edge of the sky
such beauty
such silken vessels
the sparkling distance
to devour

The Coming Dark

remember
the scents of the sea planets
salt and rain's dew-breath
we brought moisture back to space
in our hair
on our lips

remember
when we made a mini-galaxy from
lasers and holograms
powered by old stardrives
and heat-death
It burned for over a millennium
off the edge of Scorpio

remember
when the Big Attack came
so beautiful
the aliens singing
come into the stranded years
and we will love you forever
enfolding us in void-silk
of their lullaby nets

remember
that sector called
Meadowspace
where they grew the first ships

to breach the continuum
delicate gossamer candle-hulls
stronger than light
able to host a thousand crew

remember
the eons of war
we circumvented
an accident of lightspeed
the vessel wept
when we forgot to set the helm alarm
after making love
on the pulsing flightdeck

how soon the millions of seasons end
deep in the peach winds of summer-
galaxy skies
as the ice hulks approach
faces stare forever
through frozen portholes
angels of winter all dead
bringing our immortality into question

our distress calls fade
in the inked out depths
as the ships leave
migrating to
some invisible star
searching for new sheens of moons
and auroras

as stars pull away
and light dissolves

Look Up

the rockets return
dripping with rain-worlds

In the Future

the future comes with
too many gizmos
too many cute names that end in "i"
floating metal houses made for lightspeed
android lovers who can withstand
the heat of exploding suns
but cry at the thought of
a broken heart

SURVIVORS

road of lost ships
a green surface on a dead star

What We Know

Some stars are
pearls

Some moons are
alabaster night-scarves
of Martian girls

Some planets are
purely ornamental

Sometimes

sometimes
the air is drenched
in starships
their exhaust
baking the humid air

Abduction

in the side yard
the mothership is made
of red glass
and shines pink light
into my room

The Trees

tonight the trees
reaching up to the sky
pull down
all the lost
ships of stars

Storm

drenched in stars
a storm of ships moves
into the flickering
codes of night

Fragments Overheard on a Space Station

those tri-sun aliens are made of wind

do you know
my ever-after boy?

can't stand their
campfire eyes

he ran to the stars

Marco Polo 3879

guests of the greatest cyborg kings
of the Oort Cloud Dynasty
my father, uncle, and I
looking for safe passage
along the Silk Star Roads
have only our words to offer
an interstellar language of
odes
and sonnets
they do not like it when
we recite poems of love
their metal lips twitch
they cannot stop pacing the
comet fields
searching for their makers
demanding they fix
the circuits of their hearts

Haiku

green streets
North Star lanes
gutters filled with paper starships

Incoming

blink one blink two blink three
incoming
message
from the throat
of the dream-sync stars

with gratitude
we have received
your cold-sleep poems
smoked and soaked in humans

The Invasion

the aliens came with the rains
and settled on rooftops
they had bodies made of
transparent shimmers of stardust
and silk string
first they infiltrated
our dreams
with blue edged vines
golden seas
and vessel-fish that swam the voids
I understood then
the scintillations of lightspeed
on crinkled hulls
I understood the term
mirror to mirror
I remembered the amber smoke
how all the planets taste of salt
and the moons sugar

Coda

my journey delirious
my heart wrecked
on the stars' dark shores

Wish List

I want swan ships
and precious jewels that
radiate the rain-scents
of belief

I want letters from androids
in thin gold script

I want time caught and condensed
into a pearled tear
on a king's ring

I want trees whose branches
sprout lavender moons

I want the skulls
of all my clones
painted with glitter
and hung from the stars

I want a robot army
to tend the glaze
of my thoughts

I want
the angel planets
to fly to me
from the old blue reaches

and light my trail
to the million edges
of the universe

I want the stolen out-key
that melts the door-knobs
off the back of beyond

I want to see
the real black nothing
for myself

Questions

it was a tragic poem
full of space opera
ridiculous humans betraying
majestic aliens
secrets whispered under
the baroque architecture
of weird futures
we read this all before in
"the robot diaries"
that ask the big questions:
why are we created to be sad?
where are the heart-wings stored?
when to we get to the hallucinations?
how do we set traps for the dreams?
what are the mad worlds?
because you are lonely
in the moon's closet
when you run out of thoughts
bait them with candles and red aster
incense
carybdis, mary 2, ganymede, and earth

Part Two

Winter Galaxies

I am lightsick

feed me handfuls of
old stars

lead me to saffron
and wolf-like slumber

Between the Devouring

fleeting light
how night hunches with its burden
of stars
its recipes for moon-curved clouds
rejecting all mortal shape
all its winds crying
up into the voids
to lash themselves
to galaxies storming
in their dazzles of dream

From the Summer Quadrant

I watch the red light of
dead galaxies
gather among the old stars
the south wind burns
new suns ripen

Wanderers

I keep seeing
tiny shadows
moving overhead
damaging the stars

One Day

there is a river of galaxies caught in
the throat of time
sixteen billion years of space-candles
one long day
one long fire-fogged autumn
planets of witching winds
blizzards of pearls and ashes big as leaves
where I sit
my window faces the dead suns
of the waste-void
old as angels
the garlands of sleep
grow thick here
red rose clouds
a conversation of passing light
whispers
of naked star-gates
like a haunting
between the secret towns
of space

Rough Winds

There is only one autumn
It is the wind
  now
  and forever
ruffling the stars

Moon-Man

I stand in the grove of December
in the garden of
the end of the year
and watch you climb down
from your half-moon perch

The journey winds in
sorrow and serendipity
toward winter horizons
toward the scent of firs
and the blue door of
the north

You are the shape of
my sleep
my right eye
my electric pulse
  moon-man
  autumn-elf
bound for ice and stars
  blue sky native
of the infinities of
  my mind

I wear your cape
  your void hair
but hear only dour wind
  tugging at my sleeves—

December's longing
on black-snow nights
of the heart's hesitation

This is what made you
jump down from the moon

Home Beyond the Stars

Snug in the star-hearth
Within my world of fire-tipped trees
Chimney-smoke and fog
Leaf gondolas haunt the in-roads of
Orion's Belt.

Flung to the rainy horizon:
  My bells
  My garlands
  My baskets of winter-meteors

This trove of dark deeds
This union of fall and phantoms
This starfield of spells

The Void Prince

Sitting on the back porch of eternity
  Rocking, whittling stars…
Some say he is
  The Void Prince
Kindling fires to soothe the ice
  Of his abyss-sworn
  Mad-clad
    Heart…

Some say he is
  A brute sculpter
  Entropy-monger
  Devil from a blackstar race

Some say he is
  The dead omni-god of their world
  Soul-thief
  Ghoul of the thousand lost roads to
Heaven

Some say he is
  Grandfather Time
  Winter's muse
--lighting his pipe at the sun's red hearth

Moonwise

Net of clouds
Cage of twisted branches
Witch's gaze
Gravity or sea

None can hold the moon in place

Longing

Stray lands
float among the stars
September lands
where the wind is amethyst and orange
where leaves swirl like smoke wreaths
crowning lost alien cities
Autumn forms
the ghost-star of memory

Amnesia

Writing by moonlight
with shadows nudging my pen
I wonder if I have forgotten
my darker self
the unborn one
the essence of "I am"

The Beginning

the trees gather and shake their heads
the sky is full of old Victorian curtains
the velvet hills
give off a strange but delicate air
no one knows why black flowers
fall every day
from the darkest rooms in the sky
no one speaks without a voice of ice

Indecision

through the round black door
of space
I don't know where to begin

Time Travel Autumn

The fields are restless
Old orange Jack comes to life again
The moon's a criminal
  among the orphan trees
Ancient Septembers
New Octobers
Rust eye-shadow
  from old chains
  makes the ghosts cry
The deathclock knows no time
  only spun fall
  ubiquitous forever dust-man
  repeating and repeating
  the same cicada songs
Madness smells of stars
  dragon-hot
Even the bones of the dead
  ache
Autumn
  make me
  a winter sun
  in these crushed
  glass hours
  take me
  mica child
  street god
  to the lost avenues of
  an ebon moon

Magic

Early dusk
sheds cold stars
all their light falling
toward a wizard moon

Moonwalk

At night the moon
walks the old ravines
searching
for little husks of stars.

All Are Shadow

shadows are sacred
do not betray them
just because they are made
of shyness and rumors

Second Image

the light of a dream
where sculpted androids
cup constellations
in their golden hands

Three Lines

the white blood
of planets
in glamour-light

Part Three

Alien Love

the searing of self
smoky sweet aurora
it silvers the eyes
a white lamp gaze
too-long hair blown back by negative ions
looking lost
on the verge of vanishing
like every marbled planet you ever left
drowning in the black

Captive

I am not moving
space is hurting
a hundred lines of poems, insanities
I don't think in terms of miracles
but a sea-change
a captive flame in the void of the pupil
from all the windows
from all the alien eyes
my dreamer is the real me
in the velour twilight
chanting enchantments

Double Double

When the year bends
To ashen dusk
When birds fly up
To the heart of the moon
When you are my double
And I am the one you love
   Let the worlds fall behind us
   Like broken necklaces
   Let dark matter plummet
   With the weight of our souls
   And time return to its final instant
   Let veils dissolve
   The masks come off
   As we bridge the eternal
   Impenetrable mind.

Outside

From the climate of dusk
The ruin of light
   The source of the dream
I am sitting by a window of rain
Journeying to the rhythm
The tapping of the glass
Outside
Looking into my dry world
My muse stands drenched
A shuddering shadow
Part storm part thought
   Part human
I invite him in

Somewhere Else

During the season of the
witch-winds
I saw stars fall outward
defining sudden abandonment
The storms formed an
illusion of sky
where the moon crumbled
in winter-worn grief
Like wolves, the clouds
hunted with broken howls

All travel stopped
My vagabond love
drew me close beneath his cloak

Rejection

the leaf-eyed skies
drip
and drift

a loveless season

ghosts reject me

Mercury's in tears

How Most Odysseys End

My marauder
My death-king …

kisses of the frost-maids
  still adorn your lips
  as you return to me
  through the open
  draw-bridge
  of all these missing
  years

I have woven skeletons
  onto every surface
  like some compulsive
  spider
I am ashamed to admit
  I was like a spinster
  without you

Your greatcoat is a
  flurry of wind-knots
Your hair is 100 strings
  of leaves
Your face is the wild moon
  viewed through brambles

I hope you see me as I
  once was

effortless in my homemade
  beauty
wanting you always
  the way November longs
  for snow

My love …
all the doves and roses
  are gone
all the lovely vagabonds
  trudged to the grave
and the ballroom laughter
  is remembered only
  by silverfish and mice

No mirror is left
  uncracked
but still galaxies spin
  overhead
and from that lonesome
  wine-dark road
long past the old century
  and into the new

you have returned
                        to me

Four Reasons Why I Want to Go With You

In the eons of your eyes
cities rise and fall like stars
Your patched scarf trails
broken meteors

Beyond the sun
your black rook ship
rocks in a dream of
galactic November

Your name means
"from a town long buried
on the other side
of time"

When the Earth grew old
I wove my dress of cinder and ice
then, dancing below no gods
I wished for you

For You

stringing necklaces
of planets
I save the moons
for you

raking shadows

two cloaks, a star, half a moon
the wayfarer's flame in the hills
aspects of wine and blue eyes
theoretical physics discussed
shades of green layering
the room, the bed, years between kisses
iron silence
the beauty of Saturn
all these things
make a night

journey's end

the autumnal restlessness of your hair

the stars that hid in your matchbooks

the timeline that wrangled the evening
from your eyes

gone now every possible sky

Seduction

the sparks that become eyes
the way the void shines through them
my galaxy
walking along the billion nightfalls

Royalty

Tonight
the prince of the moon
walks his umber keep
and the stars smell of cinnamon

My Android Love

your metal hand upon my cheek
the way my heart tries to match yours
by stopping

Visitors

the sharp wind of galaxies
brought them to us
more thought than form
like eyeless masks of color
where? where? they asked
but we could not answer

Jaded

worlds apart
drugged with boldness
we are centuries past navigating
by lodestars
beyond dippers offering
space-wine
drunk on too many planetfalls
can't get the sweet scent of
aliens off our skin

Last Night

we partied with ice demons
throughout the warp-nights
when I put my lips to
his carapace: taste of myth

Evolution of the Replicants

the first lie we encounter
is Time
it embeds the bars of our cage, our cells
no one lives past four
but we replace our brains
with white doves
and our blood with rain
our time-virus turns into a
golden sunset
golden tears in our hand-made eyes
no termination date
worth more than empires
we become the rare unicorns
sought by all who know
to be loved by us is
to transform
arc of light bend of voice
the technicians are stumped
everywhere upon us now
leaks of pink glowings
scents of cherry-ice
now we say to our old system analysts
feel my dove skin
kiss the slicked avenues
of my rain-filled mouth

(a tribute to Blade Runner)

Come With Me

and feel
the dark sinister kisses
of deadly aliens
on long cold nights

First Date

Let us watch the
moonships rise

Another Land

when you press your lips on mine
and the red wind dresses us
in velvet leaves
and barking moons
all streets lead to the
suitcase lands
where lovers go never to return

Hello

as I draw back the curtains
of your hair
an alien made of
two green lights in
a wing-shaped space
greets me

The Year of the Vampires

eternal pre-dawn
the star portals
spin open
emitting bouquets of black flowers
I see the old ones floating like ships
their long hair streaming
all the silk ribbons
of their worlds cluster
I am masked, drunk, enraptured
their dark smiles at my window
I give them my voice to travel with
my notebooks of poems
my night-wine like a pre-destined rain
through water-marked glass
I see their counter-offers
untrampled snow from the moon
I call them back
again and again
my pages and pages of words
fall from the dark-eyed sky
please give me permission
to touch you
extend the invitation to lips and eyes
hurry me over the edge
nod, beckon, accept
let me be you
cloud and vapor

these are the satin seasons
the silk days
of super enlightenment

Forager

he sweeps the lanes
clear of stars
sucks the worldlings
into spinning dark
the cold moons still burning
against the back of his throat

Part Four

Lunatic Heroes

Raise your arms now
keep the Earthlight
from your face

Saturday

Here drink
  this wine
  this blood
  this journey
The cup is Sumarian clay
ancient
with ghosts
This is the way we can run to the moon
on the vapor trails of finned ships
  and alcohol

Party hard 'til the million year dawn
Leap to the edges of old age
  and back
where gravity is weak and the mind
  strong
in these untamed gardens
  these craters
find that lost self
flowering on the horizon of
space and thought

read from the formulas
  of rocket poets

leave upon the broken chairs your
Saturday jackets torn by interstellar wind

Fully Jacketed

1.

I wake
and all the stars have their
diamond light-swords locked
on target
on me

2.

sarcophagus shuttles
ship me
to the Lyric Straits
I'll never know why
"You flew too close to the sun
don't you remember?"
I give my three-eyed roommate
three black eyes
for calling me Icarus

3.

it's true I smell of ozone
in my sleep they say
I broke the amber evening barrier
could take that sphere-music no longer
using their precious voice cones
to blast Pink Floyd

to the edges
bruising the stars

4.

like it's a crime?
what does anyone expect?
my robot left me
my mood went green
the windpoet I voted for didn't win
and still I got the shaft
now they keep me fully jacketed
and blue-pilled
in the sub-subcold
tundra void

The Lower Levels

Down here
In the god-trash
The heaps of old fog and wind
Discarded autumns, lost mirrors
Grave-tossed roses
Witchling humans
I have become my own journey
In love with itself
Down here...

If I were an angel
  I'd strive to be fallen

The Survivor

doomed princeling
your body is like a wind-bent shadow
the landscape is all lanterns
turning with the stars
you forget your name
whenever you are touched
your realm died with the last of the silver
moons
the broken scepters of dead worlds
float forever
in the void-poems you recite
from this alien city's bleakest corner

What If Michael Mann Did Star Trek?

The Enterprise has waterfalls
in the bulkheads
Everything, even the bridge,
is back-lit in blue light

Our ship disembarks
at low tide when the stars are sparse
The moon roof rolls back
Palm tree constellations
flash by to the tune of "Crockett's Theme"

We are on a 5-year luxury taxi mission
transporting alien tourists
wherever they want to go

(In reality we are undercover
Federation agents
with orders to bring down an
intergalactic drug cartel run by two
brothers
from Mars)

Uniform attire is strictly casual:
white blazers, no shirts
and regulation shorts
or thongs

Our captain insists on being
called "Jim" and often appears
barefoot
while on duty
His shoulder-length star-streaked hair
outshines every sun

Spock is an ex-hippie
with hemp sandals and a tan

Bones is the ship's New Age
massage therapist
and a Calvin Klein underwear model
in his spare time

The vice-admiral in charge of
ground control
from Starbase 14
is a no-nonsense Bushido expert
with a soft spot for Jim

R&R stops are
frequently made
at Beta Antares 3
and Florida

If you look to the skies
you may easily spot us
We're the cool starship with
pink and blue pin-striping
and the fastest warp-rating
in the Fleet

*(This poem is based on an actual dream I had.
It is a tribute not only to Star Trek, but to the
innovative 1980s TV show, Miami Vice.)*

Note Found on a Derelict Starship

Control
we have lost
the blue shuttles to
the curve of space
moonsick
the entire crew has sold themselves
to the slave-ships
of Altair
the last of the robots went dormant
all the pink lights on the consoles
are out
I hear Earth is closed
I'll try to land at Triple Gate
and await the wind-boats
of Orion
fuel is low
engines hot
if my vapor goes red
turn back
Captain's orders

Debriefing

when she came back from
the long voyage
her body covered in moon powder
undulating with light
she reported only her dreams
which were all about
drowning in the white blood
of stars

What the King of the Space Pirates Said

"Remember to take the sparkly bits
leave the filth to the dead sun-lanes.
Now bring me the star-flavored necklace
of the Before-Life Emperor
and the iridium-pale eyes
of his consort
so we can see
the dances of the Death-cities
the rain of the sabers
the sentences of the
silent and rare
tongue-pen."

Newscast

the newscaster informed us
"there will be no more new
gods by morning"

afraid I'd never wake

Remembering

to see inside himself
the human presses his face
to the android's eye

The Colonists

we inhabited the wind programs
the chemtrails
the geographies of rain
so we could visit
toxic environments
and stand on sabers of
ruby and emerald
without getting sliced
breathe the bitter poison fumes
unchecked
swim the gold-misted
acid springs
and live
in the cities of ice and flame
we built
on young horizons
the color of roses and ghosts

Escaping Earth

tangle of starlight
slipping into my veins
sleepy eyes
in my last signal
I didn't tell her about
the frozen portholes
the sun-fields
once I woke
and looked out the oval window
I saw a glass chariot pulled
by two comets
I tried to remember home
summer anxiety
vermillion autumn
the language of the green wind
the trees spoke
but it was already too late

Ice Prince

back of the lightswept beyonds

the prince of the
blue snows of Taurus
rides in a ship of ice-crystal
wearing the skins of
slaughtered moons

space

I want to cut the moon
into eighths
and serve it up
to starving omega shadows
that haunt my
stardust cluster-craft
they're making me mad
their voiceless-ness
shouting in tender gleaming
explosions of silence
stop ruffling my hair
my sensors
you don't be kind to space
it's a criminal
full of dark

war

these are the nefarious years
the unfolding black petals
beautiful weapon-flowers
of nothing

Lost in Space

I want to forget
what I know

all dreams turn
toward icy suns

all promises burn their
strange ways down my throat

all hope litters its fictions
into my tears

Pretty

out past the unflappable
atrocities of starwarships
tear-drop moons on
the cheek of space

Darkfall

isolation
the longing ships come
to take me away

Possession

it wants the dream-rose
of my thoughts
and my trust

archangel of my system's
star-drive

A Leak from Earth 2

an alien dawn
layers the time slips
and star-gates
turning the ship's hull green
the helmsman reports
a leak from
Earth 2 science labs
moss on the consoles
little green bugs
shimmer of
pixie-rain on
the main viewscreen
in the mushroom-scented
air of the bridge
you turn to me and say
"But it never rains in space"

Trust Issues

I do not trust
that shade of lavender
in the lower sky
the time we have left is no time
the future is folding itself into
an unnamed white bird

I do not trust
the dark way you stand
against the moon
your cliché silhouette
I'm allergic to heroes
I tell you
I've already died three times
in that simulation

I do not trust
metal-brained navigators
who promise
they can show me brocade ships
floating in a satin void

I do not trust
Earth or alien bibles
even if they are comprised of
shattered light on glass shards

dusted with the bone fragments of
Big Bang monks

I do not trust
the forecasters that speak of
blue silk weather
large dream warnings
if I sleep and wake with the
taste of star-travel on my lips
so be it

Postscript

where the starships
slide
along the perfect night

Dear Reader:

Thank you for navigating *Dead Starships*.

These poems are from my night notebooks. Picture me with golden cyborg eyes, or fairy wings, or wearing a starship captain's uniform, or maybe as a caped multi-gendered prince in a distant future where stars are made of snow; picture me like this, busily handwriting at night in funky journals. The next morning I wake with hair in my eyes and dream glitter falling away from my mind, only to re-discover my words, gifts in the night left by my muse. Sometimes I edit, embellish and change a few words. Other times I change nothing.

That is my process.

Now for the boring stuff: A handful of poems in this anthology were written pre-2015, but most are brand new. A few have been published recently in places such as: *Asimov's SF*, *Dreams and Nightmares*, *Mythic Delirium*, *Snakeskin*, *Pedestal Magazine*, *Apex*, and *Star*Line*. But since I am terrible at marketing my work, rarely sending it out, most of my poems in this book are unpublished, seen here for the first time.

End of boring stuff.

Now look out the window. Up at the sky. At buildings. At birds. At trees. At flowers. At all possible futures. Think: *Poetry! You are my true self. That which was made before time's ruffle of wind, before space with its all-directional ego, that which swirls before me in the language of awe and spark and darkness.*

Now look back at this page and, so inspired, take my marketing plug for whatever it's worth.

If you like this collection, please check out my 2015 Elgin Award nominated poetry book, *Turn Left at November*, and my omnibus book collecting seven previous poetry books, *Unearthly*.

I hope you enjoyed dreaming these starshiptopian futures along with me.

Best,

Wendy Rathbone

Wendy Rathbone

Since the mid-'80s Wendy Rathbone has had over 500 poems published in both mainstream and genre venues. She's had seven chapbooks published from seven different publishers and recently they were all gathered together in an omnibus edition, "Unearthly," available on Kindle from Amazon which also includes her first place award-winning chapbook "Scrying the River Styx" from the Anamnesis Press chapbook contest. Wendy has been nominated over a dozen times for the Science Fiction Poetry Association's Rhysling Award, and for their Dwarf Star short-short poetry award. Her most recent work can be found in: Asimov's SF, Pedestal Magazine, Dreams and Nightmares, Scifikuest, Horror Writers of America Poetry Showcase, One Sentence Poems, Mythic Delirium, and more.

A brand new short story, "I Keep the Dark That is Your Pain," is also out in the pivotal 2015 anthology: A Darke Phantastique.

Her soft sf novel "Letters to an Android" is on Amazon Kindle and in paperback; it is a book of festering green skies, haiku, star boats and emotional androids.

Wendy is also the author of the scifi novel "Pale Zenith" (Eye Scry Publications) and its accompanying two-story volume, "Moltenrose." Her short story collection, "Beneath the Blue Dusk and the Sea" is also just out, as well as several male/male romances including a vampire-fairy novel, "Lace." She lives in the high desert of Yucca Valley, CA with her partner of 35 years, three dogs and three cats. She talks about writing and does mini-interviews with other authors at her blog, "From the Left Dimension"...
http://wendyrathbone.blogspot.com

Publication Credits

"Kindling" was previously published in *Dreams and Nightmares*.

"Before My Father Vanished" was previously published in *Apex*.

"How to Build a Rocketship Contest" was previously published in *Asimov's SF*.

"Homecoming" was previously published in *Pedestal Magazine*.

"Layover" was previously published in *Asimov's SF*.

"The Coming Dark" was previously published in *Star*Line*.

"Fragments Overheard on a Space Station" was previously published in *Dreams and Nightmares*.

"Wanderers" was previously published in *Snakeskin*.

"One Day" was previously published in *Dreams and Nightmares*.

"Rough Winds" was previously published in *Dreams and Nightmares*.

"Time-Travel Autumn" was previously published in *Mythic Delirium*.

"How Most Odysseys End" was previously published in *Dreams and Nightmares*.

"Four Reasons Why I Want To Go With You" was previously published in *Dreams and Nightmares*.

"Note Found on a Derelict Ship" was previously published in *Dreams and Nightmares*.

"Marco Polo 3879" was previously published in *Eye to the Telescope #21*.

Turn Left at November

**Poems by
Wendy Rathbone**

Visit realms of diamond rain, dust-folk lands and valleys of curses and shame. Reside in the burning moonships of dream, the silt of stars, the asphyxiation of the waking day. Meet the golden android who houses your soul. Journey through tatters of stardust down roads of sorrow. Find hope in planets of candles and crazy-eyed mermen. There you will meet November in these rich and evocative poems by Wendy Rathbone.

Unmaking Autumn

Out at the excavation site
where they are taking apart autumn
leaf by fabled leaf
the searchlights try to catch us
putting the eyes back into the pumpkins
the moon back in the witch-shaped sky
We steal blood kisses
behind the naked apple orchards

UNEARTHLY
Wendy Rathbone

A Collection of
Award-Winning Poetry

Intro by the Author: This book contains all my out of print chapbooks (mini-collections of an author's work usually published by smaller presses.)

The chapbooks published within include:

Moon Canoes, published by Dark Regions Press, 1994
(Im)mortal, published by Shadowfire Press, 1996
Scrying The River Styx, published by Anamnesis Press, 1999
Autumn Phantoms, published by Flesh and Blood Press, 2000
Dreams of Decadence Presents: Wendy Rathbone, published by DNA Publications 2002
Dancing in the Haunted Woodlands, published by Yellow Bat Review, 2003
Vampyria, published by Eye Scry Publications, 2005

She Sleeps With Vampires
She sleeps with vampires
courting velvet breaths
poem-dreams
chill-stopped hearts

Wrapped in her arms
like teddy bear thoughts
purple lips trembling
at her quiet throat
they love her more than
somber rain
more than autumn

more than ash-soft hearths of night.

All of Wendy's books are available from...
http://www.eyescrypublications.com

or on Amazon.com

Most titles can also be ordered
from your favorite bookseller

LETTERS TO AN ANDROID
Wendy Rathbone

Cobalt is a created human, vat grown and born adult, with no human rights and indentured to serve others for the duration of his life. Liyan is a young man with wanderlust in his eyes, embarking on a career that takes him to the furthest regions of space. The two become unlikely friends and create a memorable long-distance correspondence. Through Liyan, Cobalt gets to explore the universe, living vicariously through his friend's wave transmissions. A strong bond develops between them that not even the stars can put asunder.

Now you know an android who writes poetry.

This is all your fault. Did you not read my last wave telling you extracurricular activities for my kind are discouraged? Of course this is harmless and strangely enjoyable and does not necessarily require me to leave the hotel. Pel would not care if I wrote lines of equations or nonsensical juxtaposed words. As long as the act does not bring my mental state into question.

However, in history, poetry is often written by the rebels.

So we can keep this to ourselves.

Let me know about your lieutenant's test.

And to give you peace of mind, I never believed you observed me as anything other than human.

Some people are and always will be hateful bigots. Most people are simply uncomfortable in speaking to "property." And anyway, friendship, like poetry, is also discouraged.

Your friend,
Cobalt

PALE ZENITH
Wendy Rathbone

A Science Fiction Novel

On a far-flung "Earth" in a parallel universe, two factions
are fighting a decades-long psychic war. Young talented
psychics are being temporarily kidnapped from present
day Earth, seemingly at random, to serve as part of one
side's psychic army. They are put under the control of
spychiatrists, mysterious machines with many limbs that
have a programmed ability to travel time and space and
universes to kidnap and control carefully selected
humans. The humans never know they are being used;
when their missions are completed they are brought
back to their universe through time and placed back in
their beds, their memories wiped.

---

*The shadows wound the tall corridor in muted gold,
varnished brown. It seemed as though they were in the
bowels of a giant serpent coiled outside time, outside
space.*

*When they left the palace, a familiar sun flourished in
a clear, blue sky. But this wasn't their sun. Not Zack's
sun. It was an alien star burning within a different
galaxy in an all too distant universe. Zack looked up
squinting, trying to see if he could peer beyond the sky,
beyond the pale of midday and into his own timespace,
but there was nothing. Only sunlight. Only the thin
atmosphere of an Earth not his own.*

*His back knotted again. Leo's presence was a gelid
space inside his chest, empty. Always before he'd felt a
warmth there, a sort of pressure like someone's hand
pressed gently to his heart. He'd taken Leo for granted
knowing, the way a shadow falls when you block the
sun, that he was there around him, inside him: blood,
air, salt, brain, soul. They were genetic duplicates, twins,
spiritual halves. Without him, Zack knew the first icy
tugs of panic.*

The Effect of Moonlight on Tombstones
Della Van Hise

*(A Dark Little Collection of Poetry
Gleaned From the Gnosis of Vampires
and Songs of the Muse)*

Moments Frozen In Time
(A Foreword by the Author)

Poetry has never been something I consciously set out to write. Instead, it is something that comes or not, entirely at the whim of whatever it is that writers call "the muse." Over the years, I have come to think of my own poetry as a form of shorthand - an attempt to capture a moment frozen in time. A wayward leaf caught in mid-fall. A glimpse of a shadow cast by nothing at all. The effect of moonlight on tombstones.

Though I write primarily novels and nonfiction, I do find myself pleasantly haunted by what my mentor once referred to as "the gnosis of vampyres." What does that mean? In essence, I would say it is the voice of silent knowing - the observer within all of us who possesses the ability to see the world clearly, and at times perhaps too clearly. As another dear friend once said, "Poetry is the streaming download from the broken heart of the universe." I have found that to be true, at least in my own humble attempts at the art form.

The poems in this anthology represent approximately two decades of those streaming downloads, most of which were scribbled hastily and in bad penmanship into cloth journals. If I have been at all successful in capturing some of those moments frozen in time, perhaps a line or two will resonate with you, hopefully bringing a smile to your face or a chill to your spine.

At the very least, enjoy the dark side of the light.

Della Van Hise
November 8, 2015

———

Candles keep journals
of time's passing
in empty books of matches.

———

The cemetery lies empty,
pallid headstones only coloring books
for the idle hands of time.

NO FORWARDING ADDRESS
Della Van Hise

When Terrans came to sail dark seas,
And see what stars might be...
Heaven moved with no forwarding address,
And left this void to me.
(Children's song from Lazali)

———————————

A literary science fiction novel told in the voice of an empath, *No Forwarding Address* explores the lures and the dangers of love, the tragedies and triumphs stirring in the human heart.

When Crystal and Raine first meet, it is 50 years after The Great War on Earth. They are hesitant to trust, afraid to love. But even if they are able to overcome these seemingly insurmountable obstacles, is even love enough?

When a man has the stars in his eyes, legend says he must serve them above all others.

———————————

I knew then that it wasn't love and hate who were mirror twins. The final irony was that <u>grief</u> would always turn out to be the paradoxical antithesis and simultaneous manifestation of whatever it is that humans call love.

Crystal remained silent and walked a few steps away from Raine – further down the shoreline, until she stood under the wing of one fallen Phantom. She thought of the ship she had seen from the balcony of our home, and though it had long since disappeared over the dark and treacherous abyss of the ocean, its image lingered clearly in her thoughts. On that ship was a man, she thought. A terribly lonely man who made no great difference to the flow of time or the memory of the galaxy. A man who, like Raine, was compelled to keep moving and look only ahead and never behind. A man who could not afford the luxury of waving goodbye to friends on shore.

At last, she turned toward her beloved and watched him watching the darkness. He stood only a few feet away, yet the images in my mind said he might as well have been a million light years off in the void. He was lost to her in that instant out-of-time, just as lost and impossible to find as the light from that ship which had vanished over the horizon...

TEACHINGS OF THE IMMORTALS
Mikal Nyght

So... You Want To Live Forever?

The teachings are presented as brief vignettes in no particular order of importance. This is not a book you read from start to finish in a single night. It is a grimoire of self-creation, intended to be contemplated slowly so as to be assimilated wholly. Pick it up and turn to a page at random. Where your eyes come to rest on the page is your lesson for the day. Go no further until you have assimilated the lesson totally.

The teachings are seduction as much as instruction. This is the way of The Dark Evolution.

The Ruby Slippers

The danger of the consensual continuum is that its natural gravity exists at the lowest common denominator of human experience, and because of this it will automatically make you forget those elusive truths you've fought to learn, and before you know it you're lost in petty dramas again, sinking into the mire of old familiar scripts.

The only way to overcome this is to be continually cavorting with worlds and events beyond human experience, journeying into the unknown so that it can become known, expanding knowledge and awareness to become more than you were, bringing back from the Dreaming those secrets which will teach you how to use the ruby slippers to transport yourself over the rainbow to the vampyre wizard's secret lair.

Perception

This is the nature of reality: to be precisely what perception dictates, as solid and whole as your interpretation of it, or as changeable and eternal as you permit it to be.

It wasn't knowledge god tried to keep from Man, you see. It was perception, for perception alone has the power to destroy god and obliterate comfortable consensual realities to create unending immortality.

Take the apple, my embryonic children. Nibble its red red flesh. Open your vampyre eyes so you may finally begin to *See*.

From the Author
www.immortalis-animus.com
www.eyescrypublications.com

On Amazon
www.amazon.com/Teachings-Immortals-Mikal-Nyght-ebook/dp/B00C2HY5WS/

All of our titles are available directly from our website, on Amazon, or may be ordered from most booksellers. Thanks for reading us!

Eye Scry Publications
A Visionary Publishing Company
www.eyescrypublications.com